I AM ELSA

By Christy Webster
Illustrated by Alan Batson

 A GOLDEN BOOK • NEW YORK

I am ELSA.
I am Queen of ARENDELLE.

I was born with the power of ice and snow.

There is
beauty
in my power . . .

... but there is also **danger**.

I couldn't control my magic,
so I had to hide it.
We closed the castle gates.

I missed my sister, Anna, but
I didn't want to hurt her again.

I was afraid to become queen.

I thought people might learn my *secret*.

I RAN AWAY.

Once I was far from everyone,
I could be myself.

I built a great ice palace.

I didn't have to hide anymore.

My sister came to get me. But
I sent her away to protect her.

I was alone,
but I was free.

I didn't know that my magic had caused an eternal winter.

When soldiers came to take me home,
I tried to use my magic to **ESCAPE**.

They brought me back to the castle.

But their chains couldn't hold my magic.

In the end,
my sister
SAVED
me.

Anna's love taught me
to let go of my **FEAR**.

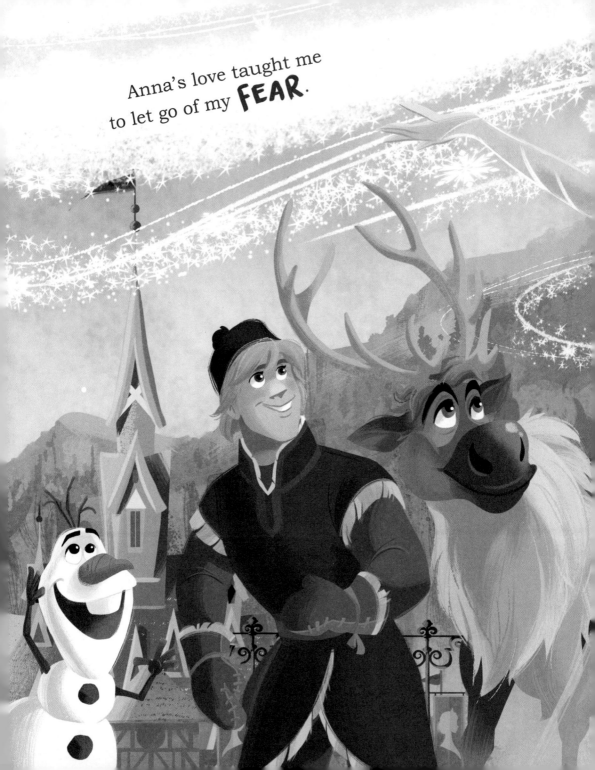

We're never
closing the
gates
again.